WAILING WELL

-FANTASY AND HORROR CLASSICS-

BY

M. R. JAMES

British Library Cataloguing-in-Publication Data
A catalogue record for this book is available from the
British Library

M. R. James

Montague Rhodes James was born in Kent, England in 1862. An intellectually gifted child, he excelled academically at both Temple Grove School and Eton College before enrolling at King's College, Cambridge. A highly respected scholar to this day, James' areas of research interest were apocryphal Biblical literature and mediaeval illuminated manuscripts. He was, by turns, Fellow, Dean, and Tutor at King's College, and in 1905 was installed as Provost. James was a highly sociable man, and he travelled widely throughout Europe.

James came to writing fiction relatively late, not publishing his first collection of short stories – *Ghost Stories of an Antiquary* (1904) – until the age of 42. Many of his tales were written as Christmas Eve entertainments and read aloud to friends. James described his introduction to ghosts in 1931: "In my childhood I chanced to see a toy Punch and Judy set, with figures cut out in cardboard. One of these was The Ghost. It was a tall figure habited in white with an unnaturally long and narrow head, also surrounded with white, and a dismal visage. Upon this my conceptions of a ghost were based, and for years it permeated my dreams." James believed that must a good story must "put the reader into the position of saying to himself: 'If I'm not careful, something of this kind may happen to me!'" He eventually published five collections of his ghost stories, all of which were reprinted and adapted numerous times.

Modern scholars now see James as having redefined the ghost story for the 20th century by abandoning many of the formal Gothic clichés of his predecessors and using more realistic contemporary settings. However, James's tales tend to reflect his own antiquarian interests, and he is seen as the founder of the 'antiquarian ghost story'. His first two collections – *Ghost Stories of an Antiquary* (1904) and *More Ghost Stories* (1911) – are generally regarded as his most important, containing as they do the well-known stories 'Number 13', 'Count Magnus', 'Oh, Whistle and I'll Come to You, My Lad' and 'Casting the Runes'.

The onset of World War One marked the beginning of the end of James' golden years in Cambridge. In 1918, he accepted the post of Provost of Eton College. He was awarded the Order of Merit in 1930, and died in 1936, aged 73.

WAILING WELL

In the year 19— there were two members of the Troop of Scouts attached to a famous school, named respectively Arthur Wilcox and Stanley Judkins. They were the same age, boarded in the same house, were in the same division, and naturally were members of the same patrol. They were so much alike in appearance as to cause anxiety and trouble, and even irritation, to the masters who came in contact with them. But oh how different were they in their inward man, or boy!

It was to Arthur Wilcox that the Head Master said, looking up with a smile as the boy entered chambers, 'Why, Wilcox, there will be a deficit in the prize fund if you stay here much longer! Here, take this handsomely bound copy of the Life and Works of Bishop Ken, and with it my hearty congratulations to yourself and your excellent parents.' It was Wilcox again, whom the Provost noticed as he passed through the playing fields, and, pausing for a moment, observed to the Vice-Provost, 'That lad has a remarkable brow!' 'Indeed, yes,' said the Vice-Provost. 'It denotes either genius or water on the brain.'

As a Scout, Wilcox secured every badge and distinction for which he competed. The Cookery Badge, the Map-making Badge, the Life-saving Badge, the Badge for picking up bits of newspaper, the Badge for not slamming the door when leaving pupil-room, and many others. Of the Life-saving Badge I may have a word to say when we come to treat of Stanley Judkins.

You cannot be surprised to hear that Mr. Hope Jones added a special verse to each of his songs, in commendation of Arthur Wilcox, or that the Lower Master burst into tears when handing him the Good Conduct Medal in its handsome claret-coloured case: the medal which had been unanimously voted to him by the whole of Third Form. Unanimously, did I say? I am wrong. There was one dissentient, Judkins mi., who said that he had excellent reasons for acting as he did. He shared, it seems, a room with his major. You cannot, again, wonder that in after years Arthur Wilcox was the first, and so far the only boy, to become Captain of both the School and of the Oppidans, or that the strain of carrying out the duties of both positions, coupled with the ordinary work of the school, was so severe that a complete rest for six months, followed by a voyage round the world, was pronounced an absolute necessity by the family doctor.

It would be a pleasant task to trace the steps by which he attained the giddy eminence he now occupies; but for the moment enough of Arthur Wilcox. Time presses, and we must turn to a very different matter: the career of Stanley Judkins—Judkins ma.

Stanley Judkins, like Arthur Wilcox, attracted the attention of the authorities; but in quite another fashion.

It was to him that the Lower Master said, with no cheerful smile, 'What, again, Judkins? A very little persistence in this course of conduct, my boy, and you will have cause to regret that you ever entered this academy. There, take that, and that, and think yourself very lucky you don't get that and that!' It was Judkins, again, whom the Provost had cause to notice as he passed through the playing fields, when a cricket ball struck him with considerable force on the ankle, and a voice from a short way off cried, 'Thank you, cut-over!' 'I think,' said the Provost, pausing for a moment to rub his ankle, 'that that boy had better fetch his cricket ball for himself!' 'Indeed, yes,' said the Vice-Provost, 'and if he comes within reach, I will do my best to fetch him something else.'

As a Scout, Stanley Judkins secured no badge save those which he was able to abstract from members of other patrols. In the cookery competition he was detected trying to introduce squibs into the Dutch oven of the next-door competitors. In the tailoring competition he succeeded in sewing two boys together very firmly, with disastrous effect when they tried to get up. For the Tidiness Badge he was disqualified, because, in the Midsummer schooltime, which chanced to be hot, he could not be dissuaded from sitting with his fingers in the ink: as he said, for coolness' sake. For one piece of paper which he picked up, he must have dropped at least six banana skins or orange peels. Aged women seeing him approaching would beg him with tears in their eyes not to carry their pails of water across the road. They knew too well what the result would inevitably be. But it was in the life-saving competition that Stanley Judkins's conduct was most blameable and had the most far-reaching effects. The practice, as you know, was to throw a selected lower boy, of suitable dimensions, fully dressed, with his hands and feet tied together, into the deepest part of Cuckoo Weir, and to time the Scout whose turn it was to rescue him. On every occasion when he was entered for this competition Stanley Judkins was seized, at the critical moment, with a severe fit of cramp, which caused him to roll on the ground and utter alarming cries. This naturally distracted the attention of those present from the boy in the water, and had it not been for the presence of Arthur Wilcox the death-roll would have been a heavy one. As it was, the Lower Master found it necessary to take a firm line and say that the competition must be discontinued. It was in vain that Mr. Beasley Robinson represented to him that in five competitions only four lower boys had actually succumbed. The Lower Master said that he would be the last to interfere in any way with the work of the Scouts; but that three of these boys had been valued members of his choir, and both he and Dr. Ley felt that the inconvenience caused by the losses outweighed the advantages of the competitions. Besides, the correspondence with the parents of these boys had become annoying, and even distressing: they were no longer satisfied with the printed form which he was in the habit of sending out, and more than one of them had actually visited Eton and taken up much of his valuable time with complaints. So the life-saving competition is now a thing of the past.

In short, Stanley Judkins was no credit to the Scouts, and, there was talk on more than one occasion of informing him that his services were no longer required. This course was strongly advocated by Mr. Lambart: but in the end milder counsels prevailed, and it was decided to give him another chance.

So it is that we find him at the beginning of the Midsummer Holidays of 19—at the Scouts' camp in the beautiful district of W (or X) in the county of D (or Y).

It was a lovely morning, and Stanley Judkins and one or two of his friends—for he still had friends—lay basking on the top of the down. Stanley was lying on his stomach with his chin propped on his hands, staring into the distance.

'I wonder what that place is,' he said.

'Which place?' said one of the others.

'That sort of clump in the middle of the field down there.'

'Oh, ah! How should I know what it is?'

'What do you want to know for?' said another.

'I don't know: I like the look of it. What's it called? Nobody got a map?' said Stanley. 'Call yourselves Scouts!'

'Here's a map all right,' said Wilfred Pipsqueak, ever

resourceful, 'and there's the place marked on it. But it's inside the red ring. We can't go there.'

'Who cares about a red ring?' said Stanley. 'But it's got no name on your silly map.'

'Well, you can ask this old chap what it's called if you're so keen to find out.' 'This old chap' was an old shepherd who had come up and was standing behind them.

'Good morning, young gents,' he said, 'you've got a fine day for your doin's , ain't you?'

'Yes, thank you,' said Algernon de Montmorency, with native politeness. 'Can you tell us what that clump over there's called? And what's that thing inside it?'

'Course I can tell you,' said the shepherd. 'That's Wailin' Well, that is. But you ain't got no call to worry about that.'

'Is it a well in there?' said Algernon. 'Who uses it?'

The shepherd laughed. 'Bless you,' he said, 'there ain't from a man to a sheep in these parts uses Wailin' Well, nor haven't done all the years I've lived here.'

'Well, there'll be a record broken to-day, then,' said Stanley Judkins, 'because I shall go and get some water out of it for tea!'

'Sakes alive, young gentleman!' said the shepherd in a startled voice, 'don't you get to talkin' that way! Why, ain't your masters give you notice not to go by there? They'd ought to have done.'

'Yes, they have,' said Wilfred Pipsqueak

'Shut up, you ass!' said Stanley Judkins. 'What's the matter with it? Isn't the water good? Anyhow, if it was boiled, it would be all right.'

'I don't know as there's anything much wrong with the water,' said the shepherd. 'All I know is, my old dog wouldn't go through that field, let alone me or anyone else that's got a morsel of brains in their heads.'

'More fool them,' said Stanley Judkins, at once rudely and ungrammatically. 'Who ever took any harm going there?' he added.

'Three women and a man,' said the shepherd gravely. 'Now just you listen to me. I know these 'ere parts and you don't, and I can tell you this much: for these ten years last past there ain't been a sheep fed in that field, nor a crop raised off of it—and it's good land, too. You can pretty well see from here what a state it's got into with brambles and suckers and trash of all kinds. You've got a glass, young gentleman,' he said to Wilfred Pipsqueak, 'you can tell with that anyway.'

'Yes,' said Wilfred, 'but I see there's tracks in it. Someone must go through it sometimes.'

'Tracks!' said the shepherd. 'I believe you I Four tracks: three women and a man.'

'What d'you mean, three women and a man?' said Stanley, turning over for the first time and looking at the shepherd (he had been talking with his back to him till this moment: he was an ill-mannered boy).

11

'Mean? Why, what I says: three women and a man.'

'Who are they?' asked Algernon. 'Why do they go there?'

'There's some p'r'aps could tell you who they was,' said the shepherd, 'but it was afore my time they come by their end. And why they goes there still is more than the children of men can tell: except I've heard they was all bad 'uns when they was alive.'

'By George, what a rum thing!' Algernon and Wilfred muttered: but Stanley was scornful and bitter.

'Why, you don't mean they're deaders? What rot! You must be a lot of fools to believe that. Who's ever seen them, I'd like to know?'

'I've seen 'em, young gentleman!' said the shepherd, 'seen 'em from near by on that bit of down: and my old dog, if he could speak, he'd tell you he've seen 'em, same time. About four o'clock of the day it was, much such a day as this. I see 'em, each one of 'em, come peerin' out of the bushes and stand up, and work their way slow by them tracks towards the trees in the middle where the well is.'

'And what were they like? Do tell us!' said Algernon and Wilfred eagerly.

'Rags and bones, young gentlemen: all four of 'em: flutterin' rags and whity bones. It seemed to me as if I could hear 'em clackin' as they got along. Very slow they went, and lookin' from side to side.'

'What were their faces like? Could you see?'

'They hadn't much to call faces,' said the shepherd, 'but I could seem to see as they had teeth.'

'Lor'!' said Wilfred, 'and what did they do when they got to the trees?'

'I can't tell you that, sir,' said the shepherd. 'I wasn't for stayin' in that place, and if I had been, I was bound to look to my old dog: he'd gone! Such a thing he never done before as leave me; but gone he had, and when I came up with him in the end, he was in that state he didn't know me, and was fit to fly at my throat. But I kep' talkin' to him, and after a bit he remembered my voice and came creepin' up like a child askin' pardon. I never want to see him like that again, nor yet no other dog.'

The dog, who had come up and was making friends all round, looked up at his master, and expressed agreement with what he was saying very fully.

The boys pondered for some moments on what they had heard: after which Wilfred said: 'And why's it called Wailing Well?'

'If you was round here at dusk of a winter's evening, you wouldn't want to ask why,' was all the shepherd said.

'Well, I don't believe a word of it,' said Stanley Judkins, 'and I'll go there next chance I get: blowed if I don't!'

'Then you won't be ruled by me?' said the shepherd. 'Nor yet by your masters as warned you off? Come now, young gentleman, you don't want for sense, I should say. What should I want tellin' you a pack of lies? It ain't sixpence to me anyone goin' in that field: but I wouldn't like to see a young chap snuffed out like in his prime.'

'I expect it's a lot more than sixpence to you,' said Stanley. 'I expect you've got a whisky still or something in there, and want to keep other people away. Rot I call it. Come on back, you boys.'

So they turned away. The two others said, 'Good evening' and 'Thank you' to the shepherd, but Stanley said nothing. The shepherd shrugged his shoulders and stood where he was, looking after them rather sadly.

On the way back to the camp there was great argument about it all, and Stanley was told as plainly as he could be told all the sorts of fools he would be if he went to the Wailing Well.

That evening, among other notices, Mr. Beasley Robinson asked if all maps had got the red ring marked on them. 'Be particular,' he said, 'not to trespass inside it.'

Several voices—among them the sulky one of Stanley Judkins—said, 'Why not, sir?'

'Because not,' said Mr. Beasley Robinson, 'and if that isn't enough for you, I can't help it.' He turned and spoke to Mr. Lambart in a low voice, and then said, 'I'll tell you this much: we've been asked to warn Scouts off that field. It's very good of the people to let us camp here at all, and

the least we can do is to oblige them—I'm sure you'll agree
to that.'

Everybody said, 'Yes, sir!' except Stanley Judkins, who
was heard to mutter, 'Oblige them be blowed!'

Early in the afternoon of the next day, the following
dialogue was heard. 'Wilcox, is all your tent there?'

'No, sir, Judkins isn't!'

'That boy is the most infernal nuisance ever invented!
Where do you suppose he is?'

'I haven't an idea, sir.'

'Does anybody else know?'

'Sir, I shouldn't wonder if he'd gone to the Wailing
Well.'

'Who's that? Pipsqueak? What's the Wailing Well?'

'Sir, it's that place in the field by—well, sir, it's in a
clump of trees in a rough field.'

'D'you mean inside the red ring? Good heavens! What
makes you think he's gone there?'

'Why, he was terribly keen to know about it yesterday,
and we were talking to a shepherd man, and he told us a lot
about it and advised us not to go there: but Judkins didn't
believe him, and said he meant to go.'

'Young ass!' said Mr. Hope Jones, 'did he take anything
with him?'

'Yes, I think he took some rope and a can. We did tell

him he'd be a fool to go.'

'Little brute! What the deuce does he mean by pinching stores like that! Well, come along, you three, we must see after him. Why can't people keep the simplest orders? What was it the man told you? No, don't wait, let's have it as we go along.'

And off they started—Algernon and Wilfred talking rapidly and the other two listening with growing concern. At last they reached that spur of down overlooking the field of which the shepherd had spoken the day before. It commanded the place completely; the well inside the dump of bent and gnarled Scotch firs was plainly visible, and so were the four tracks winding about among the thorns and rough growth.

It was a wonderful day of shimmering heat. The sea looked like a floor of metal. There was no breath of wind. They were all exhausted when they got to the top, and flung themselves down on the hot grass.

'Nothing to be seen of him yet,' said Mr. Hope Jones, 'but we must stop here a bit. You're done up—not to speak of me. Keep a sharp look-out,' he went on after a moment, 'I thought I saw the bushes stir.'

'Yes,' said Wilcox, 'so did I. Look... no, that can't be him. It's somebody though, putting their head up, isn't it?'

'I thought it was, but I'm not sure.'

Silence for a moment. Then:

'That's him, sure enough,' said Wilcox, 'getting over the hedge on the far side. Don't you see? With a shiny thing. That's the can you said he had.'

'Yes, it's him, and he's making straight for the trees,' said Wilfred.

At this moment Algernon, who had been staring with all his might, broke into a scream.

'What's that on the track? On all fours—O, it's the woman. O, don't let me look at her! Don't let it happen!' And he rolled over, clutching at the grass and trying to bury his head in it.

'Stop that!' said Mr. Hope Jones loudly—but it was no use. 'Look here,' he said, 'I must go down there. You stop here, Wilfred, and look after that boy. Wilcox, you run as hard as you can to the camp and get some help.'

They ran off, both of them. Wilfred was left alone with Algernon, and did his best to calm him, but indeed he was not much happier himself. From time to time he glanced down the hill and into the held. He saw Mr. Hope Jones drawing nearer at a swift pace, and then, to his great surprise, he saw him stop, look up and round about him, and turn quickly off at an angle! What could be the reason? He looked at the field, and there he saw a terrible figure— something in ragged black—with whitish patches breaking out of it: the head, perched on a long thin neck, half hidden by a shapeless sort of blackened sun-bonnet. The creature was waving thin arms in the direction of the rescuer who was approaching, as if to ward him off: and between the two figures the air seemed to shake and shimmer as he had never seen it: and as he looked, he began himself to feel something of a waviness and confusion in his brain, which made him guess what might be the effect on someone within closer range of the influence. He looked away hastily, to see Stanley Judkins making his way pretty quickly towards the clump, and in proper Scout fashion; evidently picking his steps with care to avoid treading on snapping sticks or being caught by arms of brambles. Evidently, though he saw nothing, he suspected some sort of ambush, and was trying to go noiselessly. Wilfred saw all that, and he saw more, too. With a sudden and dreadful sinking at the heart, he caught sight of someone among the trees, waiting: and again of someone—another of the hideous black figures—working slowly along the track from another side of the held, looking from side to side, as the shepherd had described it. Worst of all, he saw a fourth—unmistakably a man this time—rising out of the bushes a few yards behind the wretched Stanley, and painfully, as it seemed, crawling into the track. On all sides the miserable victim was cut off.

Wilfred was at his wits' end. He rushed at Algernon and shook him. 'Get up,' he said. 'Yell! Yell as loud as you can. Oh, if we'd got a whistle!'

Algernon pulled himself together. 'There's one,' he said,

'Wilcox's: he must have dropped it.'

So one whistled, the other screamed. In the still air the sound carried. Stanley heard: he stopped: he turned round: and then indeed a cry was heard more piercing and dreadful than any that the boys on the hill could raise. It was too late. The crouched figure behind Stanley sprang at him and caught him about the waist. The dreadful one that was standing waving her arms waved them again, but in exultation. The one that was lurking among the trees shuffled forward, and she too stretched out her arms as if to clutch at something coming her way; and the other, farthest off, quickened her pace and came on, nodding gleefully. The boys took it all in in an instant of terrible silence, and hardly could they breathe as they watched the horrid struggle between the man and his victim. Stanley struck with his can, the only weapon he had. The rim of a broken black hat fell off the creature's head and showed a white skull with stains that might be wisps of hair. By this time one of the women had reached the pair, and was pulling at the rope that was coiled about Stanley's neck. Between them they overpowered him in a moment: the awful screaming ceased, and then the three passed within the circle of the clump of firs.

Yet for a moment it seemed as if rescue might come. Mr. Hope Jones, striding quickly along, suddenly stopped, turned, seemed to rub his eyes, and then started running towards the field. More: the boys glanced behind them, and saw not only a troop of figures from the camp coming over the top of the next down, but the shepherd running up the slope of their own hill. They beckoned, they shouted, they ran a few yards towards him and then back again. He mended his pace.

Once more the boys looked towards the field. There was nothing. Or, was there something among the trees? Why was there a mist about the trees? Mr. Hope Jones had scrambled over the hedge, and was plunging through the bushes.

The shepherd stood beside them, panting. They ran to him and clung to his arms. 'They've got him! In the trees!' was as much as they could say, over and over again.

'What? Do you tell me he've gone in there after all I said to him yesterday? Poor young thing! Poor young thing!' He would have said more, but other voices broke in. The rescuers from the camp had arrived. A few hasty words, and all were dashing down the hill.

They had just entered the field when they met Mr. Hope Jones. Over his shoulder hung the corpse of Stanley Judkins. He had cut it from the branch to which he found it hanging, waving to and fro. There was not a drop of blood in the body.

On the following day Mr. Hope Jones sallied forth with an axe and with the expressed intention of cutting down every tree in the clump, and of burning every bush in the field. He returned with a nasty cut in his leg and a broken axe-helve. Not a spark of fire could he light, and on no single tree could he make the least impression.

I have heard that the present population of the Wailing Well field consists of three women, a man, and a boy.

The shock experienced by Algernon de Montmorency and Wilfred Pipsqueak was severe. Both of them left the camp at once; and the occurrence undoubtedly cast a gloom—if but a passing one—on those who remained. One of the first to recover his spirits was Judkins mi.

Such, gentlemen, is the story of the career of Stanley Judkins, and of a portion of the career of Arthur Wilcox. It has, I believe, never been told before. If it has a moral, that moral is, I trust, obvious: if it has none, I do not well know how to help it.